A STARLIT SNOWFALL

WRITTEN BY NEWBERY MEDALIST

NANCY WILLARD

ILLUSTRATED BY CALDECOTT MEDALIST

JERRY PINKNEY

LITTLE, BROWN AND COMPANY
New York Boston

Little, Brown and Company

Hachette Book Group
237 Park Avenue, New York, NY 10017
Visit our website at www.lb-kids.com

Little, Brown and Company is a division of Hachette Book Group, Inc.
The Little, Brown name and logo are trademarks of Hachette Book Group, Inc.

The publisher is not responsible for websites (or their content) that are not owned by the publisher.

First Edition: November 2011
Originally published in hardcover by Little, Brown and Company as
A Starlit Somersault Downhill

Library of Congress Cataloging-in-Publication Data

Willard, Nancy.
[Starlit somersault downhill]
A starlit snowfall / by Nancy Willard ; illustrated by Jerry Pinkney. —1st ed.
p. cm.
Previously published under title: A starlit somersault downhill. 1993.
Summary: Having made a plan to spend the winter with Bear napping in a cozy cave,
Rabbit finds himself too energetic to sleep and decides to join the world outside.
ISBN 978-0-316-18366-6
[1. Stories in rhyme. 2. Bears—Fiction. 3. Rabbits—Fiction. 4. Winter—Fiction.] I. Pinkney, Jerry, ill. II. Title.
PZ8.3.W668St 2011
[E]—dc22
                              2010048038

10 9 8 7 6 5 4 3 2 1

QUAL

Printed in China

The illustrations for this book were done in watercolor on watercolor paper.
The text was set in Caslon, and the display type was hand-lettered.

To my sister, Ann Korfhage
N. W.

To my granddaughter Victoria Scott
J. P.

"It is not wise," the brown bear said,
"to ask of snow your daily bread
when springs are still and berries few.
My cave is big enough for two.

"My cave's so warm, my fur so deep,
no storm shall stir us out of sleep.
And I have made a rustling bed
of moss and marsh grass, newly dead.

"Accept my shelter, rest your feet.
We two shall snore through hail and sleet
and lay aside both grass and sun
till hills go green and rivers run."

The rabbit peeked in at the door.
Dry rushes carpeted the floor.

The rabbit sighed. "How ripe and sweet
this patch of clover by my feet!
The fields are broad, the hills are wide.
A pity we should stay inside."

He leaped and lolloped, sprang and spun,
under the clover-spinning sun.

But when the frost snapped leaf and seed,
the rabbit hastily agreed.

They carried water from the spring
and laid out all the breakfast things
and washed their faces in the stream

and wished each other pleasant dreams.
They closed the cave, shut out the light,
folded their paws, and said "Good night."

The rabbit tossed and turned alone.
"O prudent friend! O sleeping stone!"

The rabbit poked his silent back.
"How I should love a little snack,
a tuft of grass, a bunch of bark,
a star to tame the lonely dark."

No cold breath blew, no blizzard howled,
but someone ground his teeth and growled.

"Some go in green, some go in white.
The snow's footfall is very light.
It is not wise for us, dear bear,
when snow combs silver from her hair—

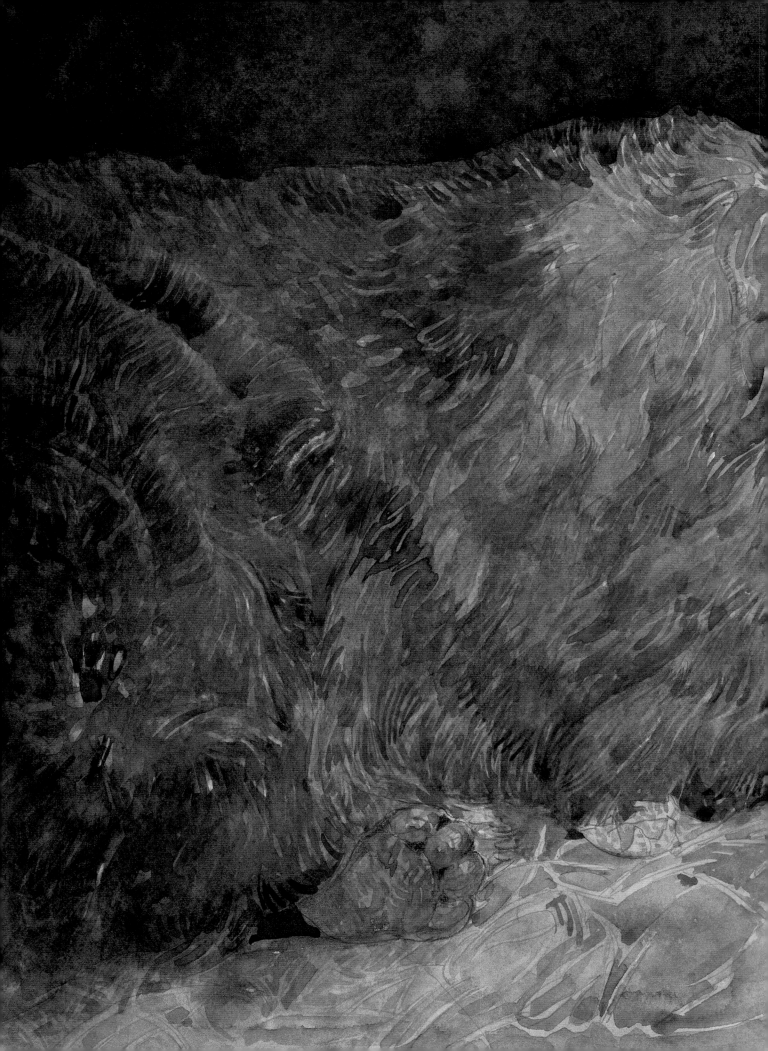

and stars are shears and hills are sheep,
it will not do to fall asleep.
How inconvenient to play dead!"

The rabbit found the door and sped

in starlit somersaults downhill

and took the snow upon his tongue
and sang, "I shall be dancing still
when hills go green and rivers run."